"Star Galaxy for the World"
a story to heal Yourself & the Planet Earth
by Della Burford

"You are the grace of the unseen, Surrender
to that and dedicate your actions to that"
(from Padma Yoga)

Thanks to the Buckminster Fuller Institute &
Design Science Studio who have made me
a coheart for 2021-2022
Editing: Dale Bertrand - Jacquie Howardson
ISBN
Azatlan Publishing
978-927825-15-0
http://www.dellaburford.com
https://www.dellaburfordartist.ca
Contact Della:
dellaburford@gamil.com

"Star Galaxy for the World"

After creating the self-healing story of "Miracle Galaxy" to help those in crisis,and seeing it performed in Japan, I realized this story should now become a story for not only to self heal but to heal the World. So"Star Galaxy for the World" was created. It shares with you the awareness, inner wisdom, transformation and beauty needed, and encouragement to take action to make ourselves and the world whole now and for the future. I give special thanks to Buckminster Fuller who I saw in Los Angles speak in 1979 where I was leading workshops for children around Dodoland at the Symposium for Humanity. When he spoke his body disappeared and he shone like a light bulb. I knew at that moment it is possible as humans to be cosmic and embraced his quote -" You are not you, you are the universe." I also embraced his idea that we should work for humanity and all living things and devoted my life to working towards this goal.

Della Burford 2021

Dedication & Thanks

To three special people in the Spirit World dear friends Adaea Smart, Desiree Burford, and my twin Donna Yerxa

Thanks to Dale Bertrand, my husband, who has been with me to collect the colors of the rainbow for decades.

Thanks to Robert Moss for his prayer before dreaming and his Dream Growing course where I developed the story with my dreams as guidance. Thanks to so many Dreamers in the course and those friends online.

Tenzin Waghal Rinpoche for this Open heart thru Gratitude Cyber Sangha & Dream Yoga.

Thanks for David Walsh for believing in me and my story and art and his kind heart.

Thanks Chris Martin for the videoing – Youtube Della Burford or dellabirdhelmet. Thanks to Glen Burford for mentoring in video.

Thanks to all those who performed Dodoland in New York and Magical Earth Secrets and Miracle Galaxy in Japan Also to friends and family who helped do the first Dream storytelling for Dale's Big Birthday. More thanks are later.

"Take me to a place of healing & empowerment"

Once upon a time there was a child called Star Child .. she was surrounded by the beauty of nature. The trees are alive, the water clear, the air fresh and the sky spacious around you. But she felt nature was being polluted. One day she did not feel well and healthy - she felt her aura was almost gone. A Covid virus has affected many people in the world and she discovered she had it. In healing she knew that her dreams would help her so that night before dreaming she made an intention: "Show me what I need to know. Please guide me to a place healing & empowerment for myself, others and our earth that is in crisis right now". To her surprise she dreams that she was in a egg shaped cell. There is a door and a window but she is in lock down and she cannot get out. Her freedom is gone. Her elders told her she must transform things from bad to good.

She say a prayer she has been taught by her elders: "May all doors, gates and passage ways to dreams be open and may all doors, gate and pathways be closed to anyone who will cause harm to me or anyone I love or the Planet Earth. And so it may be". She is told by the elder to blow away any negative thoughts. She goes to sleep and the door of the egg cell opens up in a dream, and she is met by two mermaids who said they will take her to the Star Galaxy where she is to go in four directions and find the Magic Storytellers who will give her healing balls of light. She will also hear the wise words of the Synergy Wizard. She must guard the light balls carefully and send them back to the earth for herself and and all living things that live on the Planet. She must first quickly go South.

Gratitude Storyteller

Star Child travels first to the Southern Sun Portal Gate. Here she see a Spirit Quetzal Bird who is known for living in the upper canopy of the Rainforest in a Tree House. When she goes up the Tree House she sees an incredible view of the surrounding as she is are now amongst the tallest trees. You feel such gratitude for such beauty that nature gives us.

Gratitude Storyteller says, " Receive with gratitude all you are given and feel Gratitude in your heart. We can dissolve jealousy and anger with gratitude". She also goes on to say "You must feel gratitude for the sacred living nature and grow a better and closer sacred relationship to nature. You and nature are one. Nature love an protects you and you should love and protect Nature.

She says the Magic Words are," **I and Gratitude are one, I love Gratitude, I love the Earth, I will take Gratitude Action for the myself and the Earth."She heard the Synergy Wizard say ***" Make the world work, for 100% of humanity and all life, in the shortest possible time, through spontaneous cooperation, without ecological offense...".** She got red on her aura & a ball of red light to put in her Travelling Hat. Her legs and feet feel stonger. She join others in the "Gratitude for Nature" Dance & Song. Though she feels strong in her legs and feet she still feels like her heart needs to be stronger. She is told to go and meet the Kindness Storyteller of the West Portal.
***Buckminster Fuller

Kindness Storyteller

Star Child goes to the Western Moon Gate of the Heart. The flowers talk and the Moon gives new spirit to life. The flowers say: "Grow dreams, grow them strong towards the sky. Nature is Sacred and you have a Sacred Nature to yourself too".

She is at a Magic Flower Garden. The moonlight shines on flowers of every color. There is magic as in the full moon people that can turn into Flowers when they wish and turn back into people when they want. Also in the Magic Garden at the time of the full moon any mean streaks in people are changed to self-less kindness and this how people become like flowers.

A Spirit Swan takes her to the Kindness Storyteller. The Kindness Storytellers gently says, "Every person, country, leaf, dream, idea and action is a petal on the Medicine Wheel". She says the Magic Words are : " **I and Kindness are One. I love Kindness. I love the World. I will take Kindness action for myself and the Earth.**" You hear the Synergy Wizard's words:*** "**Make the world work at the disadvantage of no one.... It has to be everybody or nobody**". She breathes in Kindness in the air all around which is the life-force. She feels compassion. She gets a green light on her aura and a green ball to put in her hat. During the day here are sacred Healing Sting-less Dream Bees buzzing all around who not only take away pollution but pollinate the flowers with their kindness. They also visit people to help them heal. Her heart feels like it is filling up again and she smiles. In Celebration she joins the "People Flower " Dance. After she is told to go North and find the Peace Storyteller.
   ****Buckminster Fuller

Wonder Storyteller

At the Eastern to Sun Gate of Beauty Star Child is told to follow the Spirit Eagle. When she does she sees a Wonder Playground. She hears the laughter of the Cockatoo Bird. There are swings to swing on, magic tricks to play, finger paints, dress up dolls, and costumes for her to put on and wear. People of any age can find the "inner child" within at the Wonder playgound.

You meet the Wonder Storyteller who tells her the Magic Words: "I and Wonder are one. I love Wonder, I love the World. I will take Wonder Action for myself and the Earth." The wise Synergy Wizard says: ***"**Never forget, no matter how overwhelming life's challenges and problems seem to be, that one person can make a difference in the world. In fact, it is always because of one person that all the changes that matter in the world come about. So be that one person.**"

She gets yellow and orange on her aura take a yellow ball of light to go in her Travelling Cloud. Her Cloud hat changes shape and looks like a jester hat. In celebration she joins the "Wonder Child" Song and Dance" with other Wonder Makers who play many instruments including drums. She feels like she is now now playing and dancing on a Medicine Wheel. Energy Wizard says : "Dare to be Naive". After she are told to go further into the Sun Gateway and meet the Magic Creativity Storyteller.
***Buckminster Fuller

Intuition Storyteller

Star Child continues along Sacred Mandala with the four Gateways . She is told to go the Northern Moon Gate of Awareness. It is night-time and she sees an Spirit Owl. The owl guides her inside the Moon Gate to an Oracle Cave. There sits a Blue Light Being radiating gold light. The Blue Light Being has a healing flower in one hand and a fruit in the other and is sitting in front of the Blue pond in the Oracle Cave. The pond reflects the power of the full moon. You see the Dream Bees , who tell her to gently massage the area in the middle of your forehead clockwise - an area which is called the Third Eye. As she is she is also to make an HUM sound . When she does the sound rings and echoes throughout the cave. From the cave she hears the words of the Synergy Wizard: ***" **It is a matter of converting our high technology from weaponry to livingry**".

The Blue Light Being says "On the Medicine Wheel you will see Visions. You have an inner eye that knows when things are right and it is called Intuition." The Blue Light Being went on to say, "Look at the full moon shining. Imagine a ball of white light ,like the moon, at your forehead and say the Magic Words, **I and Intuition are one, I love Intuition, I love the World, I will take Intuition action for myself and the Earth.**" When she looks in the 3rd eye light she knows intuitively that instead of fighting living from the heart is her important goal.

She get indigo on her aura and a indigo ball of light to put in her cloud. In Celebration she joins other people meditating and doing the "Singing Bowl" Song and Dance.
** Quote from Buckminster Fuller

Peace Storyteller

Star Child travels futher to the Moon Gate of Protection. Here she see a Spirit Blue Heron. She also hears the cooing of Peace Doves. She see a Peace Storyteller at the center of the Ancient Stone Circle where she sits and feels an inner peaceful energy. There is peace in the Medicine Wheel.

The Peace Storyteller tells her, "There is peace inside and outside. The sacred earth is our heaven so love and protect it." You are part of this so take care of yourself. She feels the blue color of the sky after sunset and feel the peace inside. She is told the Magic Words ,"**I and Peace are one, I love Peace, I love the World, I will take Peace action for myself and the world. " The Wise Synergy Wizard says: ***"We are not here to fight something or tear something down; We are here to be the example of what is possible.**"

She breathes in fresh air and it fills her with life. She gets blue in her aura and a blue ball of light to put in her hat. She feels the freshness of the air for your health and the world's health. In Celebration she join other Peace Makers who are people that turn into birds and dance the "Bird People" Song and Dance. They turn into birds like the Hummingbird, Blue Bird, Woodpecker and Crow and as they do change they become various shades of blue. She receive with gratitude a turquoise blue ball of light to put in her Travelling Hat.
***Buckminster Fuller

Creativity Storyteller

The last Gate the Star Child travels to is the Eastern Sun Gate of Abundance. Here she sees a Spirit Falcon flying above. She follow the Falcon and it takes her to a Pyramid. She is told there are many Sacred Pyramids in the World. Some in Egypt, Mexico and Guatemala. From this Pyramid comes a Magic Creativity Storyteller who has a painting of the Milky Way on her cape that represents the Goddess of the Milky Way and the Star Nations. She speaks some wise words"On the Medicine Wheel you can go the edge and look out and find the Milky Way. You are part of this Galaxy. She tells you to look out at the stars and sky gaze and this will open your body, chakras and connections. When you do you feel Spaciousness. Now you have purple on your open & you are open to receiving creativity and co-creating with the divine. The Synergy Wizard joins the Creativity Storyteller.

The Creativity Storyteller continues "**Space is outside and space is inside. What exists in the Galaxy exists in the Solar System. What exists in the Solar System exists on Earth. What exists on Earth exists in our bodies. What exists in the Galaxy exists in all living things on the Earth. Both the macro of outer-space and the micro are the same. Macro and micro are one – You are infinite - we are one. We are all one"** Creativity Storyteller also says, "When you are creative you are close to the source and the magic words are **"I and Creativity are one. I love the Creativity. I love the World. I will take Creative Actions for the Earth.** " Synergy Wizard adds, ***"**You do not belong to you, you belong to the Universe."**

Transformation Storyteller

With this the Creativity Storyteller blows on a Conch Shell. Then she gives Star Child a purple light to put in her Cloud Hat. She spirals to to the last portal going from he East is to the Centre of the Mandala. Here she meets the Transfomation Storyteller who has the wings of a butterfly. She tells the magic words: "**I and Transformation are on, I love Transformation, I love the Earth. I will take Transformation Action for the Earth.**"Star Child sees a view of the Earth from above. The Synergy Wizard says: ******There is nothing in a caterpillar to say it will be a butterfly." Star Child feels she has become a butterfly* . The Transformation Storyteller tells her"Take all the colored balls and gift them by throwing them down towards the Earth. They will circle the Earth and come back to your Travelling Cloud". When you throw the balls of light they become a rainbow around the Earth that signals the unity of people and respect and gratitude for all of nature and life.

In Celebration Star Child writes, paints and joins with other Star Wardens & Star Nation Children and Artists in the "All is One Wisdom" Song and Dance. People are doing Actions to help each other heal & the World heal. She feels creative and her aura is full and complete. Many do practical things to help the enviroment. There is more healing dreams, kindness to each other and all living things in nature.These and many more healing Actions are done to show love for nature and the planet Earth. All is well & healthy again. ***Buckminster Fuller

Miracle Galaxy Japan
Adaptation of book by – Della Burford
Production/Costumes Ruu Ruu

I am honoured to have my Miracle Galaxy (self-healing)
book made into a Storytelling Play in Japan in 2019.
Ruu Ruu has taken the Angels created for self-healing and
designed beautiful costumes and with music has told
the story. Thanks everyone there. You have inspired
me to go one step further and write and paint the story
for the World called "Star Galaxy for the World" - Della

Everyone in the the Miracle Galaxy show.
Photographs/Video by Kim Seung Yong
Peace Angel – Yuko Nawa Unui,
Kindness Angel – Momoka
Thank You Angel – Uoomin Asumi,
Willpower Angel – Noriko Akatsuka
Dream Angel – Satoko Rio Takeuchi ,
Intuition Angel – Yoko Yapak Miyauchi
Creativity Angel – Satri Abe, Wise One – Alice Yangida
Music – Mui Miyma Kono, Fairy Floss – Jo Zaczkowski

Kindness Angel – Momoka

Thank You Angel – Uoomin Asumi

Peace Angel – Yuko Nawa Unui

Music – Mui Miyma Kono, Fairy Floss – Jo Zaczkowski
with Costume Designer Ruu Ruu

Creativity Angel – Satri Abe

Dream Angel – Satoko Rio Takeuchi

Intuition Angel – Yoko Yapak Miyauchi

Willpower Angel – Noriko Akatsuka

"We - Keepers of Humanities Circle"- Vern Harper
said this to me in a dream message

1985 - Magical Earth Secrets performed in New York

Have had environmental stories storytelled and Performed since 1985. Magical Earth Secrets was done as for the Project Opportunidad in Harlem, New York City . This was before it was a book by the Western Canada Wilderness Committee.

Make an "Environmental Play" Activity

You can dance the story of "Star Galaxy for the World"

1991 – See an example: Maria Formolo Dance Co. performs Magical Earth Secrets

After seeing my (Della's) story "Magical Earth Secrets" told in a teepee, Maria decided to produce the story as a Dance and have an Environmental Event at the Edmonton Central Library. Myself and my mother, Desiree, had a collaborative show of our paintings in the lobby. Maria danced in the theatre of the library. Noreen Crone Findlay made and worked the Eagle child puppet, and Pauline Lebell sang. The production was like a dream. Thanks everyone!

Magical Earth Secrets - "Majical Rainbow" in Japan. Production Ruu Ruu, Kazuko Asaba, Costumes - Ruu Ruu, Little Eagle Child- Kazumi Oomoto, Eagle Child - Yasuhiro Zum Takeda, Mother Earth - Tara Kashahara, Earth Seed --Ricky Rusi Nishzawa, Sweetwater - Yukhi Oomoto &Satri Abe, Sunbeam - Uoomin Asami, Sun Ray - Kazyuki Mitani, Starlight - Hiromi Inti Uezmi , Lovewind - Momo Nakagawa, Starbird - Ishio Yuki, Crystal Wish - Aki Noguchi. Musicians & Friends Chie Narita, RiccaRogues Kanemura, Takuya Shimizu, Kyu Kono, Tak Suetomi, Makoto Takahashi, Bun Kalimba and Kia Isechi . Thanks also to Koseki Yuji, Hiroko Ishizuka, Hoash Kyat Yoe Hitosuki , Takuma Hara, Sho Tanishi, Naoyuki Nande, Yoko Izuhara, Tomomi Hasegawa ,Tutomi Mutaguti , Alice Yamaguchi ,Yucco, Meena Surya Sangita, Fiori Hanawo, Makoko Tsujimura, - Seung Yong Kim - thanks for the video.

Magical Rainbow - Japan Ruu*Ruu, front Tomomi Shimiza, Kazuko Asaba with Alice, Yuhki Oomoto, Satoru Ugajin, Ricky RisaNishzawa, Momoko Suda, and in the back from right to left Yuki Ishio, Masa, Yu Spring, Tazuko Noguchi, Susumu Tamura, Satri Abe, Uoomin Asami and Hiromi Inti Uezmi- missing is Yuko Nawa Inui and Fiori Hanawo the - musician. and Dan Asaba. Sorry if I have forgotten someone. Thanks everyone!

Star Galaxy for the World in Canada
Dream Storytelling for Dale's Big Birthday

Della as Narrator – Jenn and Jacquie as the Peace
Storytellers, Lucy as Transformation, Sharon at Kindness,
Jorge & Aldo – Wonder, Veronica – Creativity Storyteller,
Kelsey & Dan – Green Man & Woman, also my brother
Freeman and friends Jennifer, Nathan & Kris – Thanks

Star Galaxy for the World in Canada
Dream Storytelling for Dale's Big Birthday

Dale and Della at Storytelling in Nanaimo for Dale's Big Birthday. Below is a photo of Della with paintings done for "Star Galaxy for the World" of the Storytellers with Magic Words.

Make a Storytelling
or Play of "Star Galaxy
for the World"

I love when my stories with art are made into storytelling plays to share with many people. I have written this story to have this happen. Inspiration for this story came from the writing of my self healing story Miracle Galaxy & the Princess story . I knew now is the time to write another story to help the Planet Earth. I have also shown some historical photos for your inspiration in doing a storytelling/play of "Star Galaxy for the World". Here is a "To do" list:

1. Choose a narrator to storytell or do a reading.
2. Choose a Star Child who goes on the Journey
3. Choose seven people to be the Magic Storytellers .
When I did this in Canada for Dale's birthday we had the storytellers do an improvised version of the Magic words in sign language. We did a video of this so you can also see it. I also had the audience participate in the improvised sign langurage.
4. Choose a Synergy Wizard – we are making a puppet in Bali.
5. Make some colorful costumes.
See the photos of Ruu Ruu's costumes In Japan and the costumes I put together for the Dream Storytelling for Dale's Birthday.Since the story is a Celebration everyone can dress up!

6. Add music and dances as this is a wonderful expression of our love for the earth.
7. Follow up – make new Art to express your love for the World.

8.. Write your own poems, stories and books.
My best wishes to all –if you do please write and send photos.
If you can's do it live, do it by zoom.
              to dellaburford@gmail.com
                    ,my love Della

Dedication & Thanks

To three special people in
the Spirit World dear friends
Adaea Smart, Desiree Burford,
and my twin Donna Yerxa

Thanks to Dale Bertrand, my husband,
who has been with me to collect the colors
of the rainbow for decades.

Thanks to Robert Moss for his prayer
before dreaming and his Dream Growing
course where I developed the story with
my dreams as guidance. Thanks to so many
Dreamers in the course and those friends online.

Tenzin Waghal Rinpoche for this Open heart
thru Gratitude Cyber Sangha & Dream Yoga.

Thanks for David Walsh for believing in me
and my story and art and his kind heart.

Thanks Chris Martin for the videoing –
Youtube Della Burford or dellabirdhelmet.
Thanks to Glen Burford for mentoring in video.

Thanks to all those who performed Dodoland
in New York and Magical Earth Secrets and
Miracle Galaxy in Japan Also to friends and
family who helped do the first Dream storytelling
for Dale's Big Birthday. More thanks are later.

More Thank Yous

To Inner Council in the Spirit World: Tedrian Chyzik, Dr. Henryk Binder, Dr. Rogers, Vern Harper, Richard Pochinko, Ian Wallace, Diana Rhodes, Lyle Burford, Roman Bittman, Ava Stone, Shizuye Takashima, Buckminister Fuller, Elizabeth Kubler Ross, Dr Derek Langham, Yogi Bhajan, Dr. Dick Mazurek, Doug Riseborough, Lynne Tyrell, Bobbie Taylor, John McCleod, John Hugh Roberts,, Nicholas Roerich, David Melville, Dave Godfrey, and Incredible Red Banana.

And various Living Inner Council: Dale Bertrand, David Walsh, Robert Moss, Kazuko Asaba, Ruu Ruu, Merian Soto, Julie Lieberman, Norah Burford, Penn Kemp, Brenda, Glen Burford, David Lertzman, Karja, Brigid Marlin, Pauline Shirt, Noreen Crone Findlay, Bill Meilan, Elisa Lodge, Penn Kemp, Doug and Jules Atkins, Mary Lynne Ogilvie, Stevanne Auerbach, Dalai Lama, Tenzin Wangyal Rinpoche, I Made Sidia, Swastini, Arix ,Sugi & Peter Wilson (we are planning a dance play with the children in Bali) Tom and Sal Williams, Rolland Proulx, Brenda Parres, Virgil Scott, YasminGlanville, Pat Brennan, Kajsa Dholstom, , Laurien Towers & Aaron Zerah. Mark Jenkins, Jane Howard Baker. Michael Reed Gach, Howard & Alice Jerome, Marijke Sluitjer, Also to dear friends Mairlyn Belec, Terry Brown, Deborah Dunleavy, Sue Fox, Kathleen and Eric Bobrow, Charlyne Chiasson, Aroon and Indur Shivdasani, Gloria Arroyo, Tom und Eileen Lyons. Thanks to Dream friends: Raimonda, Meredith, Darlene, Patti, Jen, Caroline, Nana, Nanette, Holly ,Shalanhia, Lawrence, Mary Beth, Flo, Wilson, Margit, Ingrid, Becky, Cheryl , Karen, Nicole Jude, & Stephania. In the Dream Growing dream friends: Karen, Luc, Jim, Bentley, Dawn, Carol Ann, Sara, Lalenya, Cindy, Jen, Laurie, Cassandra, Moncia, Liz, Colleen, Dona, Virginia, Bob, Lisa, Denis, Dona, Bob, Lot, Virginia, Sarah, Go Kanada, Turquoise, Ann, Toni, Durelle, Claire, Sarah, Sophia - Thanks everyone!

More Thank Yous

Thanks also to Dream Friends,. And all those who performed Dodoland in New York and Magical Earth Secrets and Miracle Galaxy in Japan.

Also to friends and family who helped do the first storytelling for Dale's birthday – Lucy Mattice, Sharon Mattice, Jorge, Aldo and Veroncia, Jacquie Howardson and Jenn, and Chris Martin and Holly Yerxa. Big thanks also to Russell Coull who helped me so much when doing the final part of the story.

Also friends Bruce McCarthy, Wallace Murray and Fabrizio Belardetti & Sahara Nez, Grace Po, Francis Seaton, Susan Melville, Tom Walsh, Naomi Tyrell, Lucy and Jack, Eli and Leila Paper (Peko Li), Arnie Howardson, Jack Mattice, Evan and Eva, Paul Hugo Skywalker, Dewa Adiwisma, Rumini, Janice Klassen, Michelle Petit, Michaele Jordana, Sylke Gande, Olga Spiegel, Sorin & Leoniea, Cynthia Re Robbins, France Garrido, Irene Vincent, Rick, John, Melissa Fay, Miguel Tio, Sharlene and Victor, Jim and Pat Piercey, Irene Vincent, Benny H.V. Anderson, Andrew Gonzalez, Oleg Korolev, Brad Grigor, Edna Reti, Laurie McHale, Barbara Tremain, Mitch Gold, Ko Jason & family, Christina, Marian Hall and Elwyn Roberts and nieces Flora, and Laura & family, and nephews Chris Martin, Elissa and Dane, O.V., Michael Golland, Andrea Spalding, Sheryl McFarlane, Rob and Ewan. Myriam and family, Stella Beniuk & family, Bev Couse, To greats like Emma, Ben and Calum & Tempi, David. To the William's children Barney, Rainbow, Ollie and Liberty & their children. Thanks to Warren & Murray, Golda & Ewan. To our house mates Kelsey, Dan, Joseph & David, Nathan & Kris (former). Sorry if I forgot someone – there are many people helping me and us along the way. Thanks everyone!

Della Burford Author Page
B.Sc in Textiles, B.Ed in Art/English, N.Y.S.I.D.

Della's life is a example of dreams coming true and she encourages others to do the same. Della leads workshops internationally. A former college teacher she is a storyteller, life-long dream adventurer and author, painter of "Journey to Dodoland," "Magical Earth Secrets", "Miracle Galaxy", "Journey to a Lotus", paintings for "Spirit Storybooks", "Dream Wheels", "Art for One World", "Dream Gifts for Planet Earth" and now "Star Galaxy for the World". She facilitates many workshops in art and writing like "Creating your own Myth" and "Painting from Dreams".

Her stories have been plays such as "Journey to Dodoland." and "Magical Earth Secrets" which were performed for seven years to over 100,000 children in New York. Della co-directed these productions and was co-playwright & costume designer. Her stories have been shared in museums, schools, hospitals, prisons & at Festivals. On the internet Dodoland has been visited by 2 million people. For seven years "Magical Earth Secrets" was made into a play in Japan and now "Miracle Galaxy". The book "Miracle Galaxy" was created to help those in need face a crisis. The Galaxy itself and Mandala Spheres came to her in a dream. Della was honored to have this story shared with many cancer patients at Inspire Health and other organizations helping people with cancer. Also part of this story was shared in the "Newtown Peace Park Handbook".

In 2018 she created a book of her, Dale Bertrand, Kazuko Asaba & Ruu Ruu's life called "Art for One World" before her & Dale went to Japan to be guests at the Kanazawabunko Festival where "Majical Rainbow" was being performed. She after focused her work on the environment and completed "Dream Gifts for Planet Earth" and "Star Galaxy for the World" Remembering her dreams has helped her fulfill her true destiny in life. Della's work is for self development, our Mother Earth, all of humanity and spirit.

www.ingramcontent.com/pod-product-compliance
Lightning Source LLC
Chambersburg PA
CBHW041004170626
46815CB00002B/158